EVERYTHING GROWS

Raffi

Paintings by Eugenie Fernandes

for Felix Joseph Flynn Geuer

Raffi

for Camryn Marie

Eugenie Fernandes

Published by Rounder Books, A Rounder Records Group
Company, One Camp Street, Cambridge, Massachusetts 02140

Raffi. Everything Grows. Painted illustrations and an original
song show many different living things and their growth.
[1. Children's songs—Growth. 2. Fiction.] I. Eugenie Fernandes,
ill. II. Title.

PZ8.3.R124Co
ISBN 1-57940-097-3
10 9 8 7 6 5 4 3 2 1

Printed in Canada.

Everything grows and grows.

Babies do,
animals too.
Everything grows.

Everything grows and grows.
Sisters do,

brothers too.
Everything grows.

A blade of grass,
fingers and toes,

hair on my head,
a red, red rose.
Everything grows, anyone knows,
that's how it goes.

Everything grows and grows.
Babies do, animals too.
Everything grows.

Everything grows and grows.
Sisters do,

brothers too.
Everything grows.

Food on the farm,
fish in the sea,

birds in the air,
leaves on the tree.

Everything grows, anyone knows,
that's how it goes.
That's how it goes, under the sun.

That's how it goes, under the rain.
Everything grows, anyone knows,
that's how it goes.

Yes everything grows and grows.
Babies do,
animals too.
Everything grows.

Everything grows and grows.
Sisters do, brothers too.
Everything grows.

Mommas do,

and poppas too.

Everything grows.

Everything Grows

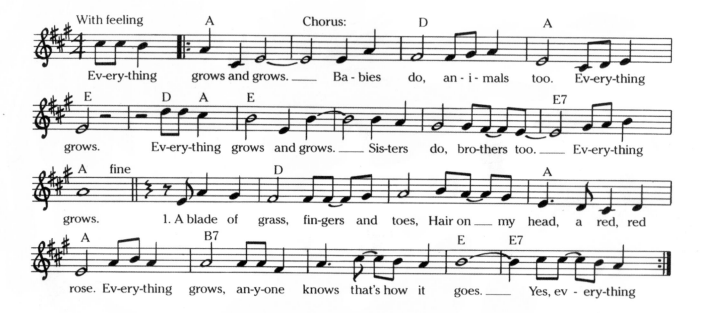

With feeling — A — Chorus: — D — A

Ev-ery-thing grows and grows. ___ Ba - bies do, an - i - mals too. Ev-ery-thing

E — D — A — E — E7

grows. Ev-ery-thing grows and grows. ___ Sis-ters do, bro-thers too. ___ Ev-ery-thing

A — fine — D — A

grows. 1. A blade of grass, fin-gers and toes, Hair on ___ my head, a red, red

A — B7 — E — E7

rose. Ev-ery-thing grows, an-y-one knows that's how it goes. ___ Yes, ev - ery-thing

2. Food on the farm, fish in the sea,
Birds in the air, leaves on the tree.
Everything grows, anyone knows,
That's how it goes.

3. That's how it goes, under the sun.
That's how it goes, under the rain.
Everything grows, anyone knows.
That's how it goes.

Words and music by Raffi, D. Pike